REVOLT AGAINST THE
ROMANS

REVOLT AGAINST THE
ROMANS

TONY BRADMAN

BLOOMSBURY EDUCATION
AN IMPRINT OF BLOOMSBURY

LONDON OXFORD NEW YORK NEW DELHI SYDNEY

Bloomsbury Education
An imprint of Bloomsbury Publishing Plc

50 Bedford Square
London
WC1B 3DP
UK

1385 Broadway
New York
NY 10018
USA

www.bloomsbury.com

First published in 2017 by Bloomsbury Education

A catalogue record for this book is available from the British Library.

ISBN
PB: 978-1-4729-2932-7
ePub: 978-1-4729-2933-4
ePDF: 978-1-4729-2934-1

2 4 6 8 10 9 7 5 3 1

Typeset by Newgen Knowledge Works (P) Ltd., Chennai, India
Printed and bound in the UK by CPI Group (UK) Ltd, Croydon CR0 4YY

To find out more about our authors and books visit www.bloomsbury.com. Here you will
find extracts, author interviews, details of forthcoming events and the option
to sign up for our newsletters.

In memory of Rosemary Sutcliff

A NOTE ON DATES

The Romans had a different way of numbering their years from us. They dated everything from the time the city of Rome was founded. So for them, the events of this story took place between the years 800 and 804 AUC (Ab Urbe Condita, which means 'from the founding of the city' in their language, Latin). We count our years from before and after the presumed date of the birth of Jesus Christ, so for us the city of Rome was founded in 753 BC (Before Christ), or what we also now call 753 BCE (Before Common Era). What happens in this story took place between the years 47 and 51 AD (Anno Domini, which is Latin for 'in the year of our Lord'), or between 47 and 51 CE (Common Era).

CONTENTS

CHAPTER ONE
A True Roman

Marcus felt his stomach fluttering with nerves as he hurried down the corridors of the villa. His father had arrived back from Rome that afternoon, and had sent a slave to find him. It seemed that Gaius Arrius Crispus wished to see his son without delay, and that couldn't be good news.

Marcus crossed the central courtyard of the house – the atrium – with its small fountain. His father's study was just beyond, the door closed. Marcus stopped in front of it, his heart pounding now too. He took a deep breath and let it out slowly. Then he knocked.

'Enter!' called his father, and Marcus did as he was told.

The study was a small square room with a window that looked out onto the hills beyond the villa and the road to Rome – a half day's ride away – which cut through them. Two walls were covered with shelves bearing thick rolls of papyrus: his father's official documents and letters. The noble himself was sitting at his desk, head bowed, closely studying a roll.

Marcus waited. 'You wanted to see me, Father?' he said after a while.

Gaius looked up. People often remarked that there wasn't much of a resemblance between father and son. Gaius was tall and thin, his face narrow and bony, his nose like the battering ram of a warship. Most of his hair was gone, and what remained was black. Marcus was stocky and his hair was light brown, like his mother's. It was said he looked like her, although he didn't know if that was true. She had died when he was very young, and he could barely remember anything about her.

'Stand straight, Marcus,' said Gaius, twisting the signet ring bearing his initials that he wore on the little finger of his left hand. 'You're slouching like a slave. And what are you wearing? That tunic has certainly seen better days.'

'I'm sorry, Father.' Marcus blushed and squared his shoulders. He never thought about what he wore when his father wasn't around, and he hadn't had time to change into something more presentable. His father set great store by appearances – his own tunic was smooth and perfectly white, even though he had ridden from Rome through the heat and dust of a summer's day.

'Well, being sorry isn't good enough, I'm afraid.' Gaius sighed. 'Sometimes I wonder what goes on in that head of yours, Marcus, I really do. Now, tell me what you've been doing since I was last here. Be sure to leave nothing out.'

Marcus relaxed a little – this was a familiar routine. He spent most of the year at their house in Rome, the great city with its temples to the gods and its streets of rich houses and its teeming slums. But he spent every summer at their villa outside the city, even though his father was usually too busy to leave Rome for more than a few days at a time.

Staying at the villa wasn't much of a holiday for Marcus. In Rome he went to school with the boys of other rich families, but in the country he was alone, with no friends of his own age to play with. He had to keep doing his lessons as well – every year his father engaged someone new as his tutor. This year's tyrant was a grumpy old Greek called Stephanos. Marcus liked some lessons more than others. He didn't enjoy mathematics, but he loved studying poetry, especially the epics from long ago. He liked *The Odyssey*, but his favourite was *The Iliad*, the great Greek poem about the siege of Troy.

'The battle scenes are absolutely amazing, Father,' said Marcus. 'Sometimes when I'm reading them it almost feels like I'm there, right beside the warriors...'

His father snorted. 'I don't think so, Marcus. I'll grant you that Homer is good on the subject of war. But believe me, there is nothing like the reality of battle.'

'No, Father,' said Marcus. Gaius knew what he was talking about. He had served with the legions before the emperor Claudius had taken him onto his staff.

'I would prefer it if you spent your time studying our country's history and its great men, such as Cato. Now *there* was a true Roman, a wonderful example to young boys.'

'Yes, Father.' Marcus felt a twinge of guilt. He often found the history of his own people quite dull, although he would never admit such a thing to his father. It seemed to be full of stories about men like Cato, who was famous for being very moral. Cato had killed himself rather than live under the rule of Augustus, the first emperor, a man whom he hated. Marcus couldn't see why that made him a hero.

'Still, I'm glad to hear from Stephanos that your Greek is excellent,' said Gaius. 'I have no doubt it will be useful to you, although frankly if it was up to me I would make everyone in the empire speak Latin like us, and nothing else.'

Marcus thought that was a strange idea – learning other tongues seemed a natural thing to do. He loved reading Homer's Greek, and speaking the language with Stephanos. Latin was the second or even third tongue for most of the villa's slaves. Marcus often talked to them too, asking questions about their countries and languages. He had even picked up a few of their words and phrases, from the Gauls especially...

'Are you listening, Marcus?' his father snapped, interrupting his thoughts.

'I'm...' Marcus was about to say he was sorry again, but stopped himself in time. 'I am, Father,' he said, but Gaius just tutted and shook his head.

'I was talking about your future, Marcus: something you never seem to consider. Oh, your studies are going well enough, but you have no self-discipline, and no idea about your responsibilities, either to me or to the empire. You're twelve now, so that must change, and luckily we have been offered an opportunity to put it right. Our noble emperor is sending me to Britannia, and you will be coming too.'

Marcus had heard of Britannia, of course. It was the empire's newest province, a distant land in the far north, across the great sea the Romans called Ocean. The emperor had conquered it a few years ago, going there to lead his legions personally in the last battles. He had returned to ride in triumph through the streets of Rome, his defeated enemies in chains behind him, their treasure heaped in wagons.

'I don't understand, Father,' said Marcus. 'What will I do there?'

'Much the same as here, but with one major difference – I will be on the staff of the governor, Publius Ostorius Scapula. So you will see from the inside how we bring the gifts of Roman civilisation to other nations. It's harder than people think to turn a land of tattooed savages into a proper Roman province. There may even be more fighting. It seems that some of the people still don't believe they've been beaten.'

He talked on, explaining what was happening in the province, listing the strangely named tribes that had accepted Roman rule, and those that hadn't. The strongest tribe in Britannia had always been the Catuvellauni, but their power had been broken during the conquest. Their chief was called Caratacus, and he had fled with his family to the western mountains where he was stirring up other tribes against Rome.

There was a great deal more – bitter feuds between the tribes, betrayals of leaders by their friends or family, appeals to Rome for help. It was all rather hard to follow, and Marcus soon found himself thinking instead of what lay ahead for him. He had never been anywhere other than Rome or the villa, and now his life was about to change completely. It was an exciting prospect, but a rather scary one too.

'When do we leave, Father?' he asked, when Gaius stopped speaking.

'I will set off by ship before the autumn storms begin. You will stay in Rome for the winter and follow me in the spring. That will give me time to find us a house, although I have no idea where. It's probably all mud huts there, apart from the camps of the legions. Still, it might do you good to spend some time with soldiers – you'll be joining a legion yourself in a few years. Now leave me – I have work to do.'

That night, Marcus lay in bed, unable to sleep... His mind was already on its way north.

CHAPTER TWO

The Savage Britons

That winter dragged for Marcus, and he could hardly believe it when the day came at last to set out on his journey. His father had arranged for him to travel part of the way on one of the emperor's ships with a group of army officers. Some were heading north to take up posts in Gaul, but several were going on to Britannia, including Quintus Flavius Sabinus, an officer who had served with Marcus's father.

'So I'll be looking after you, boy,' said Sabinus. He was a large man with a craggy face and a loud voice. 'Just do as I tell you and we'll get on fine.'

The ship was a big trireme, with three banks of oars and a sail. A pair of huge eyes was painted on the prow, and the stern-post was carved into the shape of an eagle in flight. They left Ostia, the port of Rome, early on a warm sunlit morning. The ship glided out of the great harbour, past the other ships of the emperor's fleet and the colossal warehouses where goods from all over his vast empire were stored.

Five days later they arrived in Narbo, on the southern coast of Gaul, and continued their journey northwards by land. As a senior officer, Sabinus was entitled to the use of a coach and an escort of twenty auxiliary cavalrymen. They were Gauls, as Marcus soon realised from listening to them talk – tall, strong-looking men with drooping moustaches, who rode their powerful horses as if they had been born in the saddle.

'You know the difference between auxiliaries and the legions, boy?' said Sabinus.

'Yes, sir,' said Marcus, remembering what his father had told him. 'The legions are made up of Roman citizens, the soldiers who created our empire and keep it safe. Auxiliaries are recruited from subject peoples as extra forces, such as cavalry...'

'You have been taught well,' said Sabinus. 'All credit to your father.'

Sabinus, of course, was also entitled to stay in army forts on the journey, so Marcus got to see plenty more soldiers – officers in splendid armour, centurions with their distinctive red-crested helmets, and legionaries on guard duty or saluting the eagle standards that carried the name and battle honours of each legion. The great Julius Caesar had brought Gaul into the empire almost a hundred years ago, and it had the look of a settled province. The cities Marcus passed through weren't as big as Rome, but they were built of stone and marble. Most of the people looked Roman too.

'Do you think Britannia will eventually be like Gaul, sir?' he asked Sabinus one evening at dinner. They were staying in an imperial way-station, one of the many hostels dotted along the straight Roman roads for the use of official travellers and the imperial messengers. Sabinus wasn't usually very talkative, but he had spent time fighting in Britannia, and Marcus wanted to know what he thought of it.

'I doubt it,' said Sabinus. They were sitting at a table in the dining room. The place was full of other men who were eating and drinking, or gambling with dice. 'The Britons and the Gauls are similar in some ways. They speak similar tongues, and the Gauls used to worship the same gods and have the same kind of priests. But the Britons are far more savage. The warriors tattoo their bodies and sometimes fight naked.'

A centurion at a table nearby had been listening to them. 'They collect the heads of their enemies too,' he added. The man had a hard face with a nose that had been broken more than once, and his forearms were criss-crossed with the scars of old wounds. 'Although they often just take them captive, and then hand them over to their priests – druids, they call them – for torture. I've seen some terrible things in Britannia.'

'It always seems to be cold and misty or raining there too...' Sabinus murmured, and then sighed. 'In fact, I don't mind telling you I wish I'd been posted almost anywhere else in the empire. I've fought every kind of barbarian, but the Britons are by far the worst. I only hope I manage to keep my head on my shoulders.'

The centurion laughed, and the two men talked of other countries and battles they had fought in. Marcus excused himself and went to bed, and decided not to ask Sabinus any questions in future, which seemed to suit them both.

They finally reached the port of Gesoriacum, on the northern coast of Gaul, five weeks after leaving Rome. There they transferred to another ship, and set sail for Britannia. It was a short voyage, just a day and a night, but a rough one. The sailors did a lot of praying to Neptune, god of the sea, and even sacrificed a goat to him, pouring the hot blood from its throat onto the heaving waves. But Neptune was not appeased, and Marcus was glad to arrive at Rutupiae, the main military harbour on the south coast of Britannia. It felt good to have solid ground beneath his feet again.

Sabinus took Marcus to the fort above the harbour and led him into the officers' mess while he himself went to talk to the commander.

'I hope you can ride, boy,' Sabinus said when he came back. 'Your father was supposed to meet us here, but he's been sent to Verulamium by the governor, and the only way we'll get there is by horse.'

'Oh yes, sir, I can definitely ride,' said Marcus. It was something his father had made sure he could do from an early age, and Marcus had always enjoyed it.

They stayed in Rutupiae for a night, and set out early the next morning. Sabinus looked every inch the Roman officer in his red-crested helmet and red cloak. He and Marcus had a new escort of mounted auxiliaries: twenty Batavians this time. Their homeland was on the other side of the sea, a country of marshes and rivers between

Roman Gaul and the still-unconquered barbarian tribes of Germany. 'Not much more than savages themselves,' said Sabinus, clearly not impressed. 'But we have to take what we are given.' Marcus couldn't see what the problem was – they wore round helmets and carried spears and shields, and looked tough enough to him.

The town of Verulamium lay a week's journey inland from the coast. Marcus was fascinated by the land of forests and hills and rivers they rode through. There were prosperous villages too. The people were much like the Gauls – some were dark haired, but there were many whose hair was golden or copper coloured. They wore bright clothes: the men in checked trousers and tunics, the women in red, green or blue gowns.

But none of them seemed happy to see Sabinus and Marcus and their escorts. They stayed out of their way, quickly pulling the children into their roundhouses and staring with sullen faces as the column rode past. It also rained most days, the grey sky hanging low, and Marcus felt he couldn't ever get his cloak and tunic dry, even if he sat in front of the campfires they made when they stopped for the night.

Late in the afternoon of the sixth day they forded a wide river: the Tamesis, according to Sabinus. Beyond it the track was swallowed up in a forest. The sun was hidden by a mass of grey clouds and the shadows were thick between the trees. An owl hooted and another replied, their calls echoing eerily in the still air. Sabinus frowned. He reined in his horse and raised his hand to halt the column.

'I think we should perhaps...' He never finished what he wanted to say, for suddenly a spear hurtled out of the forest and thudded into the chest of the Batavian behind him. The man looked down at it in surprise as thick blood welled up around the shaft. His eyes rolled backwards in his head and he slowly toppled sideways off his horse, crashing to the ground.

Then it seemed to Marcus that the shadows in the forest came to life and charged towards them, screaming like creatures from some terrible nightmare. But these creatures carried spears and swords and shields, and Marcus soon realised they were warriors – the savage Britons that Sabinus and the centurion had spoken of.

'Ride, boy!' Sabinus yelled, drawing his sword. 'Get out of here!'

But it was too late – Marcus was pulled from his horse and fell to the ground. A warrior stood over him, a wild, spike-haired figure wearing checked trousers, his naked chest and arms covered in swirling blue tattoos, his spear raised.

Marcus felt sure he was going to die.

CHAPTER THREE
Into the Darkness

The blow, however, didn't come. Sabinus hacked the warrior down before he could strike. The man grunted, dropped his spear and fell on top of Marcus, driving the breath out of the boy's lungs. Marcus could hear the sounds of fighting around him – the clash of blades, men yelling, horses screaming. Something warm and wet dripped onto his face, and he felt sick when he realised it was the dead man's blood. He turned his head and tried to free himself, but the body was too heavy.

Then suddenly the weight was gone, as a huge warrior with long black hair dragged away the body. This man raised his spear in the same way as the first attacker. Then another, shorter warrior grabbed the big man's spear arm and spoke to him. Marcus didn't understand what was being said, although the words sounded much like the language of the Gaulish slaves at the villa. The huge warrior shrugged and lowered his spear, then instead he roughly pulled Marcus to his feet and dragged him away.

Marcus stumbled along until he was forced to his knees. He looked up and saw that the fighting was over, and that it had been a massacre. Sabinus and all the Batavians were dead, their bodies lying in pools of blood. Some of the attackers were collecting the dead men's weapons and making separate piles of swords and spears, while others were rounding up the riderless horses. It seemed that only one of the attackers had been killed – the man Sabinus had cut down. Two warriors were kneeling beside the body, crying and chanting over it.

A tremor ran through Marcus, and his teeth began to chatter as if he were freezing cold. He could see these savage Britons more clearly now, and they were terrifying. Many of them were stripped to the waist and tattooed like the dead man, their hair sticking out of their heads in spikes like narrow blades. Marcus couldn't understand why he had been spared, but then it came to him and he shook even more. He had probably been kept alive so their priests – the druids – could torture him.

A few moments later it seemed the savages were ready to leave. More horses had been brought out of the forest, and the Britons mounted up. The captured horses had been roped together, the weapons bundled in cloaks and strapped to the saddles, and the dead savage tied across his horse. Marcus was bound with rawhide, the narrow thongs biting into his wrists and ankles. Then he was slung over a dead Batavian's horse and lashed to the bloodstained saddle, head on one side, feet on the other.

There was a sudden burst of high-pitched yelling and whooping from the triumphant

Britons. Somebody grabbed Marcus's hair and roughly yanked his head up. Another warrior was holding a man's severed head right in front of him. Marcus felt his stomach churning, bile rising into his mouth, and he was sick. The savages laughed at him now. It seemed that poor Sabinus hadn't managed to keep his head on his shoulders after all...

The sun was setting as they rode away, taking Marcus into the darkness.

* * *

There was a full moon, and they rode long into the night beneath its silvery glow. At one point Marcus was pulled from the horse and dumped on stony ground. He lay groaning, every muscle in his body aching. There was more talking above him – the huge warrior and the shorter warrior were arguing, or so it seemed. Eventually Marcus was propped up against a tree, and a sweet liquid poured into his mouth from a flask.

He slept, and when he woke up he was being put back on the horse. But this time he was sitting upright, his feet untied, his hands lashed to the pommel of the saddle. The shorter warrior mounted a horse in front of him and took Marcus's reins as well. Marcus could now see that the warrior was only a few years older than him, a boy with dark hair and an open face. He kicked his horse forward, pulling Marcus along behind him with a sudden jerk. Marcus almost fell, but managed to hold on.

That day Marcus worked out a lot of things. The Britons – he counted fifty of them – kept the rising sun directly behind them, so that meant they were heading west. They travelled quickly and avoided any villages, sticking to single-track paths and often passing through forests, so they clearly didn't want to be seen. And that meant there must be Romans somewhere nearby – perhaps they were even looking for him! Sabinus and the Batavians had probably been found by now, and the alarm raised.

They stopped earlier that night, and made camp properly. Marcus was propped against a tree once more and watched while the Britons sat around the fire, eating and drinking and talking. After a while the shorter warrior, or the boy as Marcus now thought of him, came over and offered the flask again. Marcus felt a sudden surge of anger and hatred for the savages, and refused it, turning his head away.

The boy looked angry too, and said something. Even though Marcus didn't know the words, he understood the meaning. 'Suit yourself,' the boy was saying.

'Don't worry, I will,' Marcus snapped, but the boy just scowled and stalked off.

The next day was warm, the spring sun burning through the clouds. By the time they stopped that night, Marcus was dying of thirst and gladly drank when the boy offered him the flask. He ate too, the boy giving him scraps of dried meat. Three days later they forded a river and entered a country of hills and valleys. Soon they arrived at a long hill surrounded by a ditch and a steep earth rampart, and topped by a palisade of wooden logs. They passed through a gateway into a wide space filled with roundhouses and corrals for horses, cattle, sheep and pigs. People and dogs came running up to welcome them, and most of the warriors dismounted. But the huge warrior rode on, followed by the boy and Marcus.

They came at last to a large roundhouse in the centre of the hill. Its walls were made of thick logs and a smear of white smoke emerged from a hole in the middle of its conical thatched roof. The boy dismounted and untied Marcus, and the huge warrior led him through the doorway. It was dark inside the roundhouse; the only light came from the leaping yellow flames of a fire in a ring of flat stones – the hearth. There were figures in the shadows: a fair-haired woman and two girls.

A man was sitting on a bench, staring into the fire. He wore a brown tunic and checked trousers, and his red hair was pulled back in a ponytail. Around his neck was a thick band of twisted gold that wasn't quite closed, its two ends made into the likenesses of a pair of wolves with snarling mouths. The man looked up and Marcus saw the firelight reflected in his eyes. They were pale blue, the colour of a summer sky, and his thick drooping moustache was as red as his hair.

A conversation took place, the man talking to the huge warrior and the boy. They answered him, nodding and pointing several times at their captive. Marcus tried to make out what they were saying, but could understand none of it. At last the man seemed to give an order, and the boy nodded, pulling a dagger from his belt. Marcus gasped and stepped backwards, convinced the torture was about to begin.

The man turned to him and smiled. 'Have no fear,' he said in perfect Latin. 'No harm will come to you, I swear. I have only asked Gwyn to cut your bonds.'

'But you... you speak Latin,' said Marcus, surprised. 'How can that be?'

'Some of us have learned many things from you Romans, your tongue among them. And now I wish to learn one more – what is your name?'

Marcus hesitated, but then squared his shoulders and spoke boldly, as he knew his father would wish. 'I am Marcus Arrius Crispus of Rome. Who are you?'

The man raised an eyebrow. 'Ah, you must be the son of the new arrival on the governor's staff. That is interesting. And me? Well, I have many titles – Clan Chief of the Catuvellauni, Friend of the Silures, War Leader of the Western Tribes. I am also Caradoc, son of Cunoval, although it seems your people want to steal everything from us, even our names. Your people usually call me... Caratacus.'

Marcus stared at him, hardly able to believe what he had just heard.

CHAPTER FOUR

Thirsty for Vengeance

The boy, who Marcus now knew to be called Gwyn, cut Marcus's bonds while he was distracted. Marcus rubbed the painful red weals on his wrists and thought how strange it was that he should be here, so far from home, talking to the empire's greatest enemy in Britannia. It was even stranger that the man should be so friendly, although probably that was just a pretence to make him feel at ease.

'Why have I been brought here?' Marcus said angrily. 'What do you want from me? You must want something or I would have been killed with the others.'

'You owe your life to young Gwyn,' said Caradoc. 'He saw you were not a soldier like the red-crest and his men, and he realised you might be useful to us.'

'But I don't know anything, and I wouldn't tell you even if I did,' said Marcus. 'You are nothing but a tribe of savages and I demand that you let me go...'

'It is not what you know that might be important, but who you are. Governor Scapula holds several of our people hostage. Perhaps he could be persuaded to release them in exchange for the son of one of his most trusted advisers.'

Marcus felt a surge of hope. He wondered briefly how Caradoc knew so much about the governor's staff, but that didn't matter. More important was the fact that the Britons might have a reason to keep him alive for a while yet. Then a doubt crept into his mind. 'How do I know you won't kill me anyway?' he said. 'You could tell the governor I'm alive, and then kill me once you've got what you want.'

'You must trust my word,' said Caradoc, frowning. 'We of the Catuvellauni are men of honour, and not the savage beasts you Romans think we are.'

'Really?' said Marcus. 'It seems to me only savages take the heads of men slain in battle.'

'It has always been our custom,' said Caradoc, shrugging. 'Yours is to crush whole nations, to slaughter thousands and sell the survivors into slavery.'

Marcus had no answer for that. 'So I am your hostage, then,' he said.

Caradoc's smile returned. 'Let us say rather that you are our guest, Marcus Arrius Crispus, and that we would not like you to leave just yet. I shall send a message to the governor. In the meantime Gwyn and his kin will offer you their hospitality.'

Caradoc nodded at Gwyn and the huge warrior. Gwyn came over and took Marcus by the arm, but Marcus shook him off. The huge warrior sighed and walked away, beckoning Marcus to follow. Marcus stomped after him with Gwyn behind.

And so began the days of Marcus's captivity in the Dun of the Long Hill.

*   *   *

Gwyn and his family lived in a roundhouse not far from Caradoc's. Marcus expected to be tied up again, perhaps even kept in chains like a defeated enemy, but that didn't happen. Instead he was welcomed. Gwyn's mother, a tall woman with chestnut-coloured hair and green eyes, offered him a seat by the hearth and a bowl of broth. Marcus looked at her, uncertain, but she smiled at him, so he sat and ate.

It turned out that the huge warrior was Gwyn's father, and that Gwyn also had a younger sister, a girl of six or seven who looked like her mother. Long before Marcus had finished his broth, he knew their names too. Gwyn's mother pointed at herself and said 'Alwen', and then at her husband – 'Dragorix' – and her daughter, who said 'Cati', and then blushed and ran away to hide in the roundhouse's shadows.

Alwen made up a bed-place for Marcus, a wicker frame filled with soft rushes and covered with a blanket. The family lay down to sleep not long after the sun set in a blaze of yellow and red. Dragorix looked Marcus in the eye, then nodded at the doorway and gently shook his head. Marcus knew he was being told that there was no point in trying to escape, but he was too exhausted to think about it anyway.

*   *   *

Those first few days were a very strange time for Marcus. He constantly felt on edge, worrying that the kindness of Gwyn's family was a pretence, and he was scared that he would be tortured or killed. Sleeping in the roundhouse was strange, the food was strange, being surrounded by people whose tongue he couldn't understand was strange, and strangely tiring too. And it was doubly strange to see Gwyn and his people going about their lives in ways so different from those he was used to.

The Catuvellauni hardly seemed to rest. Dragorix and Gwyn were always either mending harnesses and weapons or leaving before the sun rose to go hunting on their ponies with a pack of hounds, returning only late in the day with a brace of ducks or a small deer if they were lucky. Alwen fetched water, checked on her vegetable patch behind the roundhouse, made meals. Even Cati was occupied with small tasks, although the little girl was distracted by Marcus's presence. He often caught her staring at him, her eyes wide with wonder.

Nobody seemed to mind him wandering where he pleased. People stared at him, and said things he didn't understand, but they seemed friendly. Only once did he feel uneasy. On the second day after his arrival, the man Sabinus had killed was buried. A large crowd of men, women and children – perhaps five hundred people all told – gathered in the Dun's burial ground, a space beyond the roundhouses. The sun was sinking in the west, setting the clouds ablaze and casting long shadows.

The man was laid in a hole in the ground with a sword and spear and baskets of food and flasks of drink. A woman and three small children stood weeping beside the hole. A tall figure chanted: an old man wearing a long black robe and a headdress made of ravens' wings. At last he stopped, then spoke, angrily pointing a bony finger at Marcus. A memory came back to Marcus of the moment the warrior had died and he felt guilty – Sabinus had killed the Briton to save him.

Caradoc translated the old man's words. 'The druid Voromagos says that the Romans are to blame for the deaths of too many of our people, and that our gods are thirsty for vengeance, for Roman blood...' Marcus could feel the eyes of the crowd on him. 'But fear not, Marcus Arrius Crispus. You are more valuable to us alive than dead, so our gods will have to be satisfied with the sacrifice of a ram.'

'How long will it be before you hear from the governor?' Marcus asked.

'Who knows?' said Caradoc, shrugging. 'He is campaigning in the north, killing the people of the Parisi and burning their villages, so it may be a while yet.'

That night, Marcus sat brooding by the hearth in the roundhouse of Dragorix, staring into the yellow flames of the fire, worrying about what might happen. After a while he felt a small hand tugging at the sleeve of his tunic and he looked round. Cati was by his shoulder, looking at him with a comically sad expression, her bottom lip pushed out. She grinned and tried to push up the corners of his mouth into a smile. Marcus laughed, unable to stop himself, and saw Gwyn laughing at his sister too.

*   *   *

Life became easier for Marcus after that. He stopped thinking about the future and tried to enjoy each day as it came. It helped that he slowly began to understand the tongue of the Britons; words were suddenly becoming clear in the talk around him, like fish rising in a river from the dark depths to the surface. Cati chatted to him all the time, telling him the names of everything as if he were a baby learning to speak. Which he was, of course, at least as far as Cati was concerned.

Marcus also offered to share in whatever needed to be done – fetching water from the well for Alwen, or firewood with Gwyn. He went with Dragorix and Gwyn to the animal pens when they checked on their cattle and sheep. Their horses needed rubbing down after they had been out hunting too, and that was something Marcus knew about – he had seen slaves doing it at the villa. It was mostly Gwyn's job, and he seemed pleased when Marcus picked up a spare brush to help him.

So the days passed, the moon twice waning to nothing and waxing large again in the night sky. Then one sunlit morning, Marcus was summoned to see Caradoc. He was sitting by his hearth, just as he had been when Marcus had first met him.

'Well, we have heard from the governor,' Caradoc said softly. 'One of my riders returned with his answer late last night. He also brought this for you.'

Caradoc handed Marcus a sheet of papyrus that had been folded and sealed with wax. *How strange to see something so Roman in this place*, he thought.

Then he realised it was a letter from his father.

CHAPTER FIVE

The Council of
the Chiefs

Marcus stared at the letter for a long moment, then lifted his eyes to Caradoc's. 'So what was the governor's answer?' he said. 'Am I to be exchanged or not?'

'You are not,' said Caradoc. 'He was very clear – our people will be released only if we lay down our weapons and surrender completely to the rule of Rome.'

Marcus felt his stomach twist at Caradoc's words. The fear that he had kept at bay came rushing back to fill his heart and mind. 'I suppose this means I am no longer valuable to you,' he murmured. 'Will you let your druid sacrifice me now?'

'It is not for me alone to decide your fate. In five days there will be a gathering to discuss many important things, and we will talk about you too. But you should open the letter from your father. Perhaps something in it will make a difference.'

It suddenly occurred to Marcus that Caradoc might be able to read Latin as well as speak it. Yet he hadn't read the letter, and had handed it to Marcus unopened. Now Marcus broke the seal, with its impression of his father's signet ring, and unfolded the papyrus. There was very little writing inside it, just a few lines.

From Gaius Arrius Crispus at the Camp of the Ninth Legion at Lindum, to Marcus Arrius Crispis, his son.
Hail!
I have been told that you are in the hands of the barbarians. I give you a father's advice – do not shame your family or your emperor, and follow the example of Cato.

It was only on the second reading that his father's meaning truly sank in. For a moment he wondered if he was dreaming, if this was some terrible nightmare that would vanish when he woke up in his room at their house in Rome or at the villa. But then a cold wave of anger filled him and he crumpled the letter in his fist.

'My father thinks I should kill myself, like a true Roman,' he said.

'I am very sorry to hear that...' said Caradoc, a look of surprise on his face. But Marcus wasn't interested in what the chief of the Catuvellauni thought.

He tossed the letter into the fire and strode out of the roundhouse.

* * *

Not even Cati could put a smile on Marcus's face that night. He took to his bed and pulled the blanket over his head, refusing to respond when she tugged at it or spoke to him. Alwen brought him a bowl of broth, but he didn't touch it and eventually they left him alone. He fell asleep after a while, but then he had nightmares full of disturbing visions – Voromagos pointing at him, Sabinus's severed head...

Marcus woke with a start in the darkened roundhouse. He lay still, listening to the slow breathing of Gwyn and his family. After a while he rose quietly from his bed-place and went outside. A three-quarter moon cast a cool silvery glow over the sleeping Dun. The gates were closed for the night, a pair of warriors standing guard above them on the palisade walkway, and one gave Marcus a friendly wave.

Marcus walked on, past the roundhouses, the animal pens and the burial ground, and reached the rampart on the opposite side from the gates. He climbed up a ladder to the walkway and stood looking at the hills fading into the distance. His father was out there somewhere, although Marcus had no idea if he was looking in the right direction. But wherever his father was, Marcus had a feeling that he wouldn't be thinking about him. The noble Gaius Arrius Crispus had abandoned his son to his fate.

Of course he should have expected it, Marcus told himself. His father had never really shown him much care or paid him much attention, other than to tell him off for looking scruffy or not working hard enough at his lessons. Still, it had hurt to see from the letter just how little Gaius felt for him. But then that was the Roman way, at least as far as his father was concerned. The sons of important Roman men were brought into the world to serve their families and the state, not to be loved.

The moon faded, the sky gradually growing light in the east, the sun climbing above the hills, its blood-red rays spilling over the land. At last Marcus heard the soft clopping of hoofbeats behind him, and someone giving a low whistle. He looked round and saw Gwyn and Dragorix on their hunting ponies, with half a dozen excited hounds beside them. Gwyn was holding the reins of another pony, saddled and ready to ride.

The boy smiled and nodded at the spare mount. 'It is a good day to go hunting,' he said, and Marcus felt a flush of pleasure because he understood every word.

He smiled back and climbed down from the palisade to join his friends.

*   *   *

Dragorix and Gwyn took Marcus hunting the next day, and the day after that, and he loved every minute of it. Riding through the countryside, the thrill of the chase – it was more than enough to keep his mind empty, at least for most of the time. He was sure Caradoc had told his hosts what had happened, and that they were doing this to help him. Alwen and Cati went out of their way to be gentle with him as well.

One morning Marcus came face to face with Voromagos. The druid glared and pushed him out of the way, almost knocking him over, and Marcus felt fear touch his heart once more. He knew his future was still to be decided, and it occurred to him that the druid might well have a say in what happened. If he did, Marcus began to think he might be doomed to have his throat cut as a sacrifice after all.

Two days later the 'gathering' took place. Marcus hadn't known what to expect, but it turned out to be a big occasion. People arrived at the Dun from early morning – men on horses, women and children in carts – everyone dressed in their very best clothes. The men wore gold bands at their throats – Marcus had learned they were called torcs – and silver brooches to fasten their cloaks, and the women wore gold chains and bracelets. The warriors carried their best weapons too: spears trimmed with the feathers of eagles or hawks, and shield rims polished until they shone.

A great feast was held in the open air, with whole sheep and pigs roasted over firepits. Caradoc's wife – Marcus now knew she was called Brianna, and her daughters were Talwyn and Seren – organised the event. Everyone was eating and drinking, and children were running around having fun. Marcus sat watching, thinking of his father talking about the Britons being 'tattooed savages'. It was true, they did look strange and savage to Roman eyes, but now Marcus could only see them as... people.

'Come, Marcus,' said Gwyn after a time. 'Caradoc has summoned you.'

Gwyn and Dragorix went with him to Caradoc's roundhouse. The chief was sitting at his hearth, a dozen other men with him. They were talking and laughing, but fell silent when Marcus approached and stood in front of them. The druid Voromagos was at Caradoc's side, and stared at Marcus with a look of intense dislike.

'Welcome to the Council of the Chiefs,' said Caradoc, speaking in Latin. 'Let me introduce you – this is Conor, chief of the Silures, and this is Bedovir, chief of the Ordovices...' He gave each man's name, and they nodded solemnly at Marcus. 'We have talked of you,' Caradoc went on, 'and Voromagos has persuaded some of us here that you should be sacrificed, and your head sent to Governor Scapula.'

Marcus felt sick and wondered what he could possibly say to save his life. But Gwyn suddenly spoke up, talking angrily, a stream of words that Marcus could barely follow pouring from the young Briton's mouth. Voromagos rose to his feet, shouting and pointing at Marcus, and Dragorix stepped forward to come between them. The big warrior spoke too, his deep voice booming, and Voromagos sat down again.

'It seems you might have to thank Gwyn for saving your life a second time,' said Caradoc, smiling. 'He has bravely spoken for you against Voromagos.'

'Thank you!' said Marcus, turning to Gwyn. But Gwyn still seemed tense.

'You are not safe yet, however,' said Caradoc. 'The Council must be of one voice on such a matter.' He looked round at the other men, and they all shrugged their agreement. Voromagos scowled and gave a great sigh, but even he nodded at last. 'Good,' said Caradoc. 'That is what I wished for you, Marcus Arrius Crispus. I will arrange for you to be taken to a place where you will find your people.'

'I'm not sure if they are my people any more,' said Marcus, his words surprising him. But it felt good to say them. 'In fact... I think I want to stay here.' Then he realised that most of the Council might not understand what he was saying, and he switched from Latin to their tongue. But this time he was definite. 'I want to stay.'

Gwyn grinned, and clapped him on the back, almost knocking him over.

And so began the days of Marcus's new life in the Dun of the Long Hill.

CHAPTER SIX
Bearing the Pain

A year passed, and there came a time when Marcus could barely remember he had ever been Roman. He learned to speak the tongue of the Britons as well as he could speak Latin. He outgrew his old Roman tunic and Alwen made him new clothes, so he dressed like a Briton as well. And he ran with Gwyn and the other boys of the Dun, exploring the hills and woods and getting into all kinds of mischief.

It was always good to come home to the roundhouse, though, to eat the food that Alwen cooked, to talk with her and play with Cati. But one evening, when they had finished their meal, Dragorix turned to Marcus, a serious look on his face.

'I have something important to tell you, Marcus,' he said. It was summer and the hut was warm, but Marcus felt a chill run down his spine. 'Alwen and I have been happy to give you a place here with us, and I am sure Gwyn and Cati feel...'

'Spit it out, husband!' said Alwen. 'Can't you see that you're worrying him?'

'What? Oh, yes...' said Dragorix, who was happier with a spear or a tool in his hand than when he was talking. 'Marcus, we'd like to adopt you as our son.'

'That means you'll be my brother!' yelled Cati, jumping on his back.

'Mine too,' said Gwyn with a grin. 'Although I'll still be the oldest.'

Cati stuck her tongue out at Gwyn, and Alwen tutted. 'What a horrible pair you are!' she said. 'So, Marcus, do you think you can put up with them, and us?'

Marcus nodded, not trusting his voice, hot tears prickling in his eyes, and Cati planted a huge kiss on his cheek. Two full moons later, at the gathering for Samhain, the autumn feast, Dragorix stood before the people of the Dun and told them that Marcus was now a son to him, a bond of kinship never to be broken. A great cheer went up and Caradoc stepped forward to welcome Marcus into the tribe.

* * *

Another year passed, and Marcus began his warrior training with Dragorix and Gwyn, learning to use a spear and sword and shield. He took to it quickly, and could soon hold his own against anyone of his age, and some a lot older. He became one of the Dun's best hunters too – good at moving without being heard. He killed a wolf on his own one cold autumn day, and gave the thick pelt to Cati for her bed-place.

And in the depths of that winter, on the longest night of the year, Marcus became a man. He stood stripped to the waist by the hearth in Caradoc's roundhouse, with Dragorix and Gwyn and a crowd of other men looking on. Voromagos chanted and prayed to the gods of the tribe. Marcus had learned their names – Lugh, the god of shining light, Camulos, the god of war, Epona, the goddess of fertility. Then the druid opened a small box and took out a set of needles and a pot of blue liquid.

'Remember, not a sound,' said Voromagos, the fire reflected in his eyes. 'Bear the pain of the needles silently or you will forever be a boy. A *Roman* boy...'

'Get on with it, Druid,' said Marcus. 'And make sure my pictures are good.'

The men laughed and whooped. Voromagos glared at them, then dipped a needle into the liquid and jabbed it hard into Marcus's chest. But Marcus smiled, and kept smiling as Voromagos jabbed and scraped and wiped away the beads of blood so he could see what he was doing. It took a long while, but finally Marcus's chest and shoulders were covered with an intricate pattern of swirling blue lines. He knew what they meant – they were the symbols of the tribe, and charms to ward off harm.

'So am I a man of the Catuvellauni now?' he asked, staring at Voromagos.

'You'll do, I suppose,' said the druid with a smile, and the men cheered.

There were gifts for Marcus – a pair of war spears from Dragorix, a beautiful hunting knife from Gwyn, and a fine sword from Caradoc. But the best gift of all was a place in Dragorix's war-band. Marcus thought his heart might burst with pride as he rode out with them for the first time, beside his father and brother and the other warriors. He felt that he was as far from Rome as it was possible to be.

But Rome was coming ever closer to him.

* * *

At the time of Marcus's capture, the Romans had been pushing west, continually harassing Caradoc and his allies. Caradoc had struck back, sending small war-bands on raids into Roman-controlled territory. Then Governor Scapula had turned his attention elsewhere, and had left Caradoc alone. Now it seemed that the governor had finished things in the north, and had turned his eyes to the west once more.

Caradoc summoned another Council of the Chiefs, and Marcus went to it with Dragorix and Gwyn and the other important men of the tribe. It was a cold wet day in early spring, and they were glad of the fire that burned in Caradoc's hearth, casting shadows on the walls of the roundhouse.

'Are you sure he's got the northern tribes under control?' said Conor of the Silures, a great bear of a man with a shaggy pelt of black hair that hung down his back. 'The Parisi have never been strong, but I can't believe he's beaten the Brigantes.'

Marcus had heard of the Brigantes. Their lands straddled the northern mountains that some called Britannia's backbone, and they had a reputation for being very fierce. But most people seemed more interested in the fact that the tribe was ruled by a warrior queen. Cartimandua was her name, and she was said to be a difficult woman, although Alwen said that was just because men were afraid of her.

'He hasn't beaten the Brigantes,' said Caradoc. 'But he doesn't want to fight them and us at the same time, so he's promised to leave them alone if they stick to their own lands.'

'We all know what a Roman promise is worth,' said Bedovir of the Ordovices, a squat man with a scarred face, his eyes glittering in the firelight. 'Nothing.'

There was a murmur of agreement among the men, and for a moment Marcus wondered if anybody distrusted him. But Dragorix squeezed his shoulder, and Marcus breathed more easily. Of course everyone there had heard the story of how his Roman father had treated him, and they knew where his loyalty lay now.

'Perhaps Cartimandua will have to find that out for herself,' said Caradoc. 'In the meantime we have to deal with what is happening – Scapula attacking us.'

'But it's only been raids by his auxiliaries so far, hasn't it?' said Conor.

'Yes, he's just making sure that we don't raid them first,' said Bedovir.

'No he isn't,' said Caradoc, shaking his head. 'Scapula is no fool. He's probing – testing our strength and keeping us from discovering the route he plans to take with his legions when the time comes. But that is exactly what we need to know...'

Eventually, after more discussion, the Council agreed to send out as many war-bands as possible to do some probing of their own. Dragorix led his men from the Dun at dawn the next morning. Marcus felt a thrill of excitement as they rode through the gateway, their weapons and harnesses chinking, the hooves of the horses splashing through puddles of mud. Gwyn rode beside him with a huge grin on his face.

'It is a fine thing to ride against our enemies,' said Gwyn. 'Is it not, brother?'

'Save your breath,' said Marcus, grinning back. 'You're going to need it.'

So began a time of hard riding and fighting. Dragorix took the war-band deep into the eastern lands controlled by the Romans, and several times they came up against detachments of auxiliaries. These encounters quickly turned into skirmishes, the Britons keen to fight, but on each occasion the auxiliaries broke off and slipped away. Dragorix was wary of ambush, and never let the war-band go after them.

'Our task is to discover their plans, not take their heads,' said the big man.

Marcus couldn't decide if he was glad of that or not. The fighting had been both exciting and terrifying. Each encounter had gone by in a flash of movement and noise, of horses smashing into each other and men yelling and blades crashing into shields. In one fight he had felt a sword blade whistle past just above his head and had slashed back at his opponent, but he had no idea if he had drawn any blood.

Then one afternoon near a wooded hill they came up against some auxiliaries who were olive-skinned and wore chain-mail, baggy trousers and helmets with nodding plumes of black feathers. Marcus found himself in a duel with one, their horses side by side, and this time he felt his sword blade bite into flesh. The man swung his horse around and rode off through the trees, with Marcus following.

They hadn't gone far before the auxiliary fell from his horse. Marcus reined in his own mount and stood above the man, ready to finish off his victim, but he was already dead. Then Marcus heard a noise, a steady thud-thud-thudding of booted feet, and he walked to the edge of the wood. A column of men in helmets, some with red crests, was marching along the valley below.

The legions were coming.

CHAPTER SEVEN
Taking the War-Trail

Marcus quickly remounted and rode back to tell Dragorix what he had seen. The fight was over and the auxiliaries had gone, leaving two of the war-band dead and six of their own. Dragorix went to see the legions for himself, taking Marcus and Gwyn with him. They stood quietly in the shadows beneath the trees, watching. The Romans were still marching past, a river of men with no beginning or end, sunlight glinting on their weapons and armour and the eagle standards.

'It looks like two full legions,' murmured Dragorix, his eyes scanning the Romans, 'with plenty of auxiliary support and enough supplies for a long campaign...'

It should have been a three-day ride back to the Dun, but the war-band made it in two. Caradoc was in his roundhouse and listened carefully to what Dragorix said. Then the chief took a charred stick from the hearth and started scraping lines in the packed earth of the roundhouse floor. Marcus realised he was drawing a map.

'This is the great River Sabrina,' said Caradoc, pointing to a curved line. 'West of the river lie the mountains, and the lands of the Silures in the south – that's where the legions you saw were heading. But there are reports of another Roman force of the same size that is aiming for the Ordovices, whose lands are north of those of the Silures. The Dun of the Long Hill stands here, between the two great western tribes.'

'Do you think Scapula intends to destroy them first?' said Marcus.

'Yes, Marcus, I do,' Caradoc said quietly. 'Then he will come for us.'

'So what shall we do?' said Gwyn. 'We can't just sit and wait for him.'

Caradoc stared at his map, frowning and saying nothing for a moment. 'You are right, Gwyn,' he said at last. 'Our backs are to the mountains and the Romans are in front of us. We have no choice but to take the war-trail in opposition to them, and for that we will need a great army. Not just the Silures and the Ordovices and those of the Catuvellauni who remain free, but the other tribes too, if we can persuade them...'

The Council of the Chiefs was summoned, and Conor and Bedovir came with all their warriors, so they clearly agreed with Caradoc. Messengers were sent further afield, and before long warriors from other tribes began to arrive at the Dun of the Long Hill, as the army gathered. Most of them had fought each other in the past, but feuds and hatreds were put aside in the face of Rome, the common enemy.

The Dun grew crowded and noisy. Blacksmiths worked without rest, their anvils ringing as they pounded red-hot metal with their hammers. They forged new sword and spear blades and mended old weapons. Some men feasted and drank and swore to stand by their friends until death and beyond. Others sat quietly, talking to their wives and children, or spent their time alone, polishing shield rims and sharpening blades.

Each tribe brought its own druids, and the priests passed among the warriors like great ravens, in their black cloaks and strange feathered headdresses, praying and casting spells. Marcus and Voromagos were friends now, but seeing the druid making sacrifices to the gods so they would give his people victory sent a shiver down the boy's spine. He decided it certainly wasn't a good time to be a goat or a lamb.

Caradoc spent most of his days with the other chiefs, making plans, but in the evenings he feasted with the warriors. It was high summer now, the days full of sun, the nights warm, and they ate outside, sitting round great fires where whole pigs and cows were roasted. People laughed and joked, and one night a warrior sang a song of ancient battles, a tale of heroes who had fought each other long ago.

Marcus listened, enchanted, his mind suddenly full of Homer's poetry: those scenes of battle in *The Iliad*. The memories made Marcus wonder whether grumpy old Stephanos was still alive somewhere, being horrible to another Roman boy. Then Marcus thought of his Roman father, and realised Gaius Arrius Crispus might still be in Britannia, helping to plan Caradoc's defeat.

'This could be our last chance, Marcus,' Caradoc said quietly. Marcus had been lost in his own thoughts and hadn't seen the chief sit down beside him. 'We might be able to chase Rome from our lands forever if we can defeat Scapula now.'

Marcus turned to look at Caradoc. 'What happens if we don't?' he asked.

'I think you already know that,' said Caradoc, glancing at his wife and daughters. They were sitting on the other side of the fire, talking and laughing. Sparks rose into the night, and

Marcus was suddenly aware of the darkness surrounding the Dun.

'I do,' he murmured, thinking of the reports that had been coming in. The legions were burning villages as they marched west, slaughtering the old and any younger men who had failed to join Caradoc, and enslaving the women and children. That was the Roman way, of course, as Marcus now knew. Rome offered free peoples a hard choice – accept that you have been conquered, or be utterly destroyed.

Marcus hated the idea that Alwen and Cati might be sold into slavery. The slaves at his father's villa had always been reasonably well treated, especially the women. Yet even so, the few who had tried to run away had quickly been caught and punished, usually by being whipped and branded in front of the rest. And Marcus knew also that there were owners far more brutal than his father. And men who were taken as slaves might end up working in the salt mines, or chained for life to the rowing benches of a trireme, or even fighting as gladiators in the arena.

'But we are not finished yet, Marcus,' said Caradoc, smiling, 'so you can stop looking so gloomy. We will have a great army, and we will be like a wolf pack fighting to protect its young. It might turn out that Rome will regret coming to these islands...'

Marcus stared into the red heart of the fire, and didn't answer.

He only hoped Caradoc was right.

* * *

Three days later the army was ready to ride out. The warriors lined up in the open field beyond the Dun's gate, a mass of men on snorting horses, the early-morning sun glinting off swords and shields and the leaf-shaped blades of spears. Both men and horses were impatient to get going, but there were still farewells to be made. Women and children came running to say goodbye to husbands and fathers, brothers and sons.

'I wish Caradoc would let me come with you,' said Cati, looking up at Marcus on his horse, her small hand on his foot. 'I'd soon see off those horrible Romans.'

'I'm sure you would,' said Marcus, smiling. 'But then you would put us men to shame, so it's better if you stay and protect the Dun. And Mother, of course.'

'Hey, not so much of that, Marcus!' said Alwen. 'I know how to use a spear.'

She was smiling too, but Marcus knew she was deadly serious. A few of the older men and the young boys were staying behind to guard the Dun from any raids, and a lot of the women would be part of the same force. Marcus felt pretty sure that any Roman legionary or auxiliary who tried to hurt Cati wouldn't live very long.

'Just remember what I told you, Wife,' said Dragorix, who wasn't smiling. He towered over her on his horse, a huge figure stripped to the waist like many of the warriors, Marcus included, his muscles lithe under his blue tattoos.

'I will, Husband,' said Alwen, her eyes fixed on his, some message passing between them. Dragorix nodded and kicked his horse forward, reaching down to ruffle Cati's hair as he passed her. Gwyn did the same, and Marcus followed the two of them.

They joined the rest of the army, which had now formed into a column. Dragorix was to ride beside Caradoc at the front, with Gwyn and Marcus and the rest of the war-band, which was a great honour for them all. At last Caradoc gave the order to leave. A warrior raised a great horn-trumpet bound with gold and silver and blew into it, the blaring sound like a giant bull roaring as it charged. Other horns replied, men whistled and cheered and the horses stepped forward proudly, tossing their manes.

Marcus felt a surge of pride himself as the column moved out. It felt good to be a warrior of the Catuvellauni going on the war-trail. Then he thought of that exchange between Dragorix and Alwen, and it was like a shadow passing over the sun.

'What did Father mean?' he said to Gwyn. 'What must Mother remember?'

Gwyn turned in his saddle to look at him. 'Nothing much,' he said, shrugging. 'Just what to do if the Romans beat us and he is killed. He wants Mother to take Cati north, to friends of ours in the far lands beyond those of the Brigantes, and we are to meet them there.'

Marcus held Gwyn's gaze for a moment, then glanced over his shoulder back at the Dun. A line of older men stood on the palisade, spears raised in salute. Below them the women and children were watching the column, Alwen and Cati at the front. They looked small and distant already, and soon Marcus could see them no more.

He gripped his spear and urged his horse onwards.

CHAPTER EIGHT
Death to the Romans!

They rode north along the western bank of the Sabrina, to a place where the great river could be forded. Then they headed east, moving as quickly as they could. Caradoc's plan was simple – he wanted to attack each Roman force separately.

'That will give us the advantage of numbers,' he explained. They had stopped for the night and made camp on a hill. Marcus was standing with the chiefs and the leaders of the war-bands outside Caradoc's tent, listening to him. The rest of the army was sitting around campfires.

'We have to strike fast and hard,' Caradoc went on. 'And we have to make sure Scapula does not bring together all four legions into one force.'

But that was easier said than done. Scapula sent out lots of auxiliaries as scouts ahead of his forces. Caradoc countered with the warbands, and for a few days Marcus lived in the saddle, getting into skirmishes with auxiliaries, chasing them off, and trying to keep an eye on the northern Roman force at the same time. Then news came at last that both Roman forces were turning towards each other.

'Scapula is a wily old fox,' muttered Dragorix at the council Caradoc called that night. 'Some of his scouts must have seen us, and he has guessed your plan.'

'Yes, it is too late to stop him uniting his legions now,' murmured Bedovir of the Ordovices. 'They are the jaws of the wolf, and we will be the wolf's prey.'

The army had made camp again, this time in an ancient abandoned Dun, a hill fort with a meadow in front of it descending to a river and a dark forest beyond. The Dun's earthen ramparts were still solid, but there was no palisade topping them.

'Well then, so be it,' Caradoc said quietly. He looked around the circle of men, his eyes finally coming to rest on those of Marcus. 'It is time to stand our ground.'

'What, here?' said Conor of the Silures. 'This is where you mean to fight?'

'It is as good a place as any,' said Caradoc. 'We just need to make some preparations.'

Caradoc gave orders for all that he wanted done, and work began before the sun rose the next morning. The men collected rocks and used them to make the Dun's ramparts higher. In the meadow they dug long ditches that were deep enough to swallow men and horses. Then they filled them with sharpened wooden stakes and covered them with branches cut from the forest so they couldn't be seen.

Marcus spent the day with Gwyn and a few other men of Dragorix's war-band, scouting beyond the forest. They returned late that evening, swimming with the horses across the river then riding up to the Dun as the sun set in a blaze of fire. Caradoc was sitting on his horse, a powerful chestnut stallion, in front of the Dun's gate, his eyes fixed on the darkness in the east, with the sky blood-red behind him. It was an image that Marcus knew he would never forget.

*　*　*

The Romans came at sunrise the next morning.

The waiting warriors heard them long before they could see them, the thud-thud-thud of their marching feet filling the world like the sound of some huge beast's heart beating. Caradoc ordered the warriors to form up in battle lines in front of the Dun, while a small force was kept inside to look after the horses. The battle would be fought on foot, and the horses would be used only to pursue a defeated enemy.

Dragorix's war-band stood in the centre of the front line, with Marcus and Gwyn on either side of its leader. Marcus looked left and right at the thousands of warriors standing in line. Like him, many were stripped to the waist, their hair teased into spikes or braided. Most carried shields and spears, although some, like Dragorix, were armed with only a sword. All were grim-faced and silent, staring at the forest.

Voromagos and the other druids stood in front of the warriors, holding their arms up to the sky and chanting prayers, calling on the gods to give them a great victory. Marcus shivered and felt sick, his stomach churning with fear, but he was determined not to show it. Eventually the thud-thud-thudding stopped, swallowed by the forest, and it seemed for a long while as if everyone was holding their breath.

Then a flock of startled birds burst upwards from the forest canopy, shattering the peace. Marcus could hear rustling now and he gripped his spear more tightly. He gazed at the shadows between the trees, remembering the day Sabinus and the Batavians had been slaughtered. And suddenly the Romans appeared from the darkness, thousands of legionaries noiselessly stepping out of the forest.

The warriors before the Dun exploded into noise, yelling curses, screaming war cries and brandishing their weapons. The Romans took no notice, concentrating instead on quickly forming their own lines, a solid mass of men between the forest and the river, their helmets and shields and the eagle standards glinting. Behind them was a cluster of red-crested officers, one of them sitting on a pure white horse.

'Scapula,' Dragorix snorted, and Marcus knew he must be right. As he looked, Marcus saw the Roman governor hold up his right hand. Great bronze trumpets were raised on high in the Roman ranks, their harsh braying clearly the signal to advance. The Romans moved forward as one, the thud-thud-thudding of their hob-nailed sandals making the ground shake, their armour and weapons chinking.

Marcus knew that Caradoc had assumed the Romans would find it difficult to get across the river, his plan being to attack them as they struggled in the water. But the Romans had brought a dozen prepared bridges with them, whole tree trunks trimmed and lashed together. Teams of soldiers dragged them forward and threw them down, and their comrades swarmed across to continue their advance.

Dragorix turned to look back at Caradoc, who was sitting on his horse behind the warriors, with Conor and Bedovir and the other chiefs around him. Caradoc had seen what was happening, and now he raised his spear, pointing it at the Romans to signal the attack. The horn-trumpets of the Britons brayed now, answering the Romans. Dragorix grinned and raised his sword, the bright sun flashing off its blade.

'*DEATH TO THE ROMANS!*' he screamed, and charged down the slope.

Marcus sprang forward with everyone else, making sure he didn't fall in any of the concealed ditches, his feet pounding on the grass, his eyes on the Roman line ahead. He screamed too, a wordless war cry that was lost in the noise around him. Caradoc's warriors were like a great wave rolling in from the sea, and just before they arrived Marcus saw the Roman shields snap closer together like a giant clam closing.

Then the wave crashed into the Romans, and the fighting began. Marcus smashed his shield into a Roman one, and jabbed furiously with his spear, trying to find a gap through which he could strike the man behind it. The Romans jabbed back, their spears and swords flashing out from between their shields like the tongues of deadly snakes. Blood spurted and splashed, and warriors fell.

For a while it was all noise and fury, the warriors hacking and stabbing and trying to break through the Roman shields. But the Roman line stayed solid, and soon it began to advance again, steadily pushing the warriors back, making them bunch up against the men behind them. Marcus fought on, his breath coming in ragged gasps, his spear-arm aching, the grass churning into slippery blood-stained mud beneath his feet.

At last he realised that the line of warriors was retreating more and more quickly. The men beside him were turning to run, their faces filled with fear.

'Stop, you fools!' he heard Dragorix yelling, 'If you run we will lose...'

But it was too late. Most of the men who hadn't been slaughtered by the Romans were running now, streaming back to the Dun. Marcus was swept along with them, the Romans still moving forward, a huge monster of metal that was killing everyone in its path. Then he saw Dragorix, and pushed and shoved his way through to him.

The big warrior was standing inside the Dun's gateway with Gwyn and a few men from the war-band. Caradoc was there too, and he was arguing with Dragorix.

'I will not flee, Dragorix,' he was saying. 'If the time has come to die...'

'No, you *must* flee,' said Dragorix. 'The struggle will go on so long as you are free. I will rally enough men to hold the Romans so you can escape. What's left of my war-band will provide your escort – that includes you, Gwyn and Marcus.'

'But Father, we can't leave you here!' said Gwyn, his face a mask of anguish.

'You can, and you will,' said Dragorix. 'There is no time for farewells – the horses are saddled and waiting. May the gods protect you on your trail.'

Then he charged out of the gate with his sword raised high, screaming for the men there to follow him. Some did, and the sound of battle grew more intense.

Marcus didn't stop to think. He turned and ran with Caradoc and Gwyn to the horses.

CHAPTER NINE
The Warrior Queen

In the end they had to fight their way out of the Dun's rear gate. Scapula had released his auxiliaries, and they swiftly rode around on both sides of the Dun to cut off any escape routes. Caradoc drew his sword and charged at them, Gwyn and Marcus and the rest following behind. The auxiliaries were taken by surprise, but fought back, and Marcus found himself in a running battle, with blades clashing and men dying.

Then it was all over and Caradoc's small band burst through, leaving the auxiliaries behind. Caradoc led his men west and they rode hard, glancing over their shoulders for pursuit, not stopping until they could no longer hear the sounds of battle. Even so, they paused only long enough to catch their breath and to let the horses do the same. Caradoc soon moved them on, taking a steep track that would lead into the hills.

Two days later, on a bright warm morning, they rode up a slope to a ridge from where they could see the Dun of the Long Hill. Rising from it was a tall column of black smoke, and Marcus realised that the roundhouses were burning. There was a cluster of Roman defenders around the gate, and others scattered throughout the Dun. Legionaries stood as sentries along the ramparts.

'There is nothing here for us any more,' said Caradoc, his face stony. He roughly pulled his horse's head around and rode away, most of the small band following him. Only Marcus and Gwyn stayed on the ridge, their eyes fixed on the Dun. Marcus thought of how it must have been when the Romans had arrived – the courage of the few defenders, the fear and panic of those too old or young or weak to fight.

'Do you think Alwen and Cati got away?' Marcus asked after a while.

'I am sure of it,' said Gwyn, although there was no certainty in his voice. 'Just as I am sure that we will all meet again some day. Come, brother – we have far to go.'

Marcus, however, couldn't tear his eyes away from the burning, ruined Dun. He had spent the happiest days of his life there, and now Rome, which had already abandoned him, had taken that from him too. But after a while he pulled his horse's head around, and he and Gwyn rode after the others.

There were tears on Marcus's cheeks, and he didn't wipe them away.

*　*　*

They rode north, avoiding villages, dodging Roman patrols and keeping to the high places or the forests. Sometimes they met people – shepherds or farmers, and on one occasion a travelling merchant – and asked for news. That was how they discovered that most of the army had been slaughtered at the battle, Dragorix among them. He had killed a dozen Roman legionaries, it was said, but they had cut him down in the end. It was no surprise, but it was still hard news for Gwyn and Marcus to bear, and they were glad of each other's company that night.

They learned later that Caradoc's wife and daughters had been captured by the Romans when the Dun of the Long Hill was attacked. Marcus and Gwyn asked about Alwen and Cati, but nobody knew if the Romans had taken them too. Scapula had also put a price on Caradoc's head – a huge sum of gold would be paid to whoever brought him in chains to the governor.

'That was only to be expected,' said Caradoc, shrugging. 'And I doubt Scapula will harm my wife or daughters yet – they are too valuable to him as hostages. He will leave it a while, then threaten to kill them if I do not give myself up.'

They were in the rocky hills of the north, a dozen tired men sitting around a campfire, huddling in their cloaks for warmth. It was a chilly autumn night, the cold wind rustling through the tops of the trees a promise of the winter that was to come.

'Would you do what he wants?' said Marcus. 'Would you surrender to save them?'

'They are dead already, Marcus, even though they are still breathing.' There was a look of the deepest sadness in Caradoc's eyes. 'Dragorix was right, of course – our only hope is to keep fighting until we are dead ourselves, or can fight no more.'

'But we are so few,' said Gwyn. 'How can we keep fighting the Romans?'

'We must build a new alliance,' said Caradoc. 'And that is why we will be riding even further north. Cartimandua of the Brigantes is our only hope now.'

* * *

It was a hard journey through a land of steep bare hills and rocky passes and wild streams tumbling over tall, sharp-edged cliffs. The days grew shorter, and the wind colder, but they struggled on. One morning they saw a lone rider watching them from a distant ridge, a warrior with eagle feathers in his hair. Before long they realised they were being observed constantly, and followed too, by a whole war-band.

'It seems we have an escort,' said Caradoc. 'Those are Cartimandua's men.'

At last the trail took them into a deep valley with high hills on either side. Halfway up the slope at the far end of the valley stood a log palisade with a gate, and a great hall visible beyond. Warriors lined the walkway on the palisade, but the gate was open and Caradoc rode though it, with Marcus and Gwyn and the others following. They found themselves in a wide courtyard, where more warriors were waiting.

The doors of the hall were open, and now a woman emerged from the darkness inside. She was tall, with long black hair that hung down on either side of a striking face, and her eyes were the blue of mountain ice reflecting the winter sun. Her gown was a deep red, and around her pale throat was a necklace of bones and beaks and claws. A dagger with a silver handle hung in a scabbard from her belt.

'Welcome to my stronghold, Caradoc of the Catuvellauni,' she said. 'We have been expecting you. Come into my hall and eat, and warm yourself by my fire.'

'I give you my thanks, Cartimandua of the Brigantes,' said Caradoc, bowing his head to her. 'We have ridden far, and it is good to be with friends at last.'

That evening, Caradoc sat beside the warrior queen at her high table in the torch-lit hall, the two of them talking. The rest of Caradoc's men sat further down the table, and for a while Marcus was too busy eating to take notice of anything. But once his stomach was full, he began to look around. There were others seated with them, Cartimandua's counsellors and all the important men of the Brigantes, and they were friendly enough. But her warriors stood around the walls, watchful and unsmiling.

'They don't seem to like us,' Marcus whispered, nudging Gwyn beside him.

Gwyn looked up from his bowl at the nearest warrior. 'Maybe,' he said with a shrug. 'But then we don't have to like each other to fight the Romans, do we?'

Marcus knew Gwyn was right, of course, and tried to relax, but that was almost impossible. He had become used to seeing threats and danger everywhere, and something about the way the warriors were looking at them made him uneasy.

After a while Cartimandua rose from her seat. 'I will think on what you have asked me, Caradoc,' she said with a cold smile, the kind in which only the lips move. 'I will ask for the advice of my counsellors too, and we will speak again tomorrow.'

Caradoc bowed his head, then her warriors led him, Marcus, Gwyn and the others to a guest house behind the hall. It was large and comfortable, with a big fire in the hearth, but

Marcus noticed that Cartimandua's warriors stood on guard outside...

*   *   *

Five days went past, and each day Caradoc spoke with Cartimandua, trying to persuade her to join with him in the great fight against the Roman invaders. Then each evening in the guest house Caradoc would say something to give hope to Marcus and Gwyn and the others. 'Cartimandua is slowly coming round to our way of thinking,' he said at last, smiling at them. 'I have nearly convinced her, I can feel it...'

That night, Marcus was woken by the sound of banging on the door and loud voices. He sprang from his bed-place and saw that Caradoc and Gwyn were already standing by the door with their swords drawn. He grabbed his own weapon and stood with them, just in time to see the doors crash open. Cartimandua's warriors rushed in, and for a moment there was chaos as men yelled and struggled with each other.

Marcus fought two warriors, cutting one down before he was knocked over from behind. His sword was ripped from his grasp, his arms were brutally pulled behind his back and his wrists tied tightly. Then he was dragged outside and made to stand with Caradoc and Gwyn and the others, who were all bound in the same way. In front of them stood a line of warriors, some holding torches, the flames red against the night sky.

Then the line parted and Cartimandua walked through, a Roman officer at her side, the light of the torches glinting off his red-crested helmet and gleaming armour. Behind them Marcus could see more Romans, legionaries in full battle gear.

'Traitor!' Gwyn hissed. 'Your have sold our only hope for Roman gold.'

'Oh, this is about more than gold,' said Cartimandua. 'And there was never any hope against the might of Rome – Caradoc should have realised that long ago.'

Marcus glanced at Caradoc, who stared at her but said nothing.

Then the Romans took them away.

CHAPTER TEN
An Offer Is Made

They were thrown into the back of a wagon pulled by a team of four oxen, with the legionaries marching in front and behind, and Marcus soon realised they were being taken south. To begin with he wondered why the Romans hadn't just executed them then and there in Cartimandua's stronghold. But after a while he heard some of the legionaries talking, and everything became clear.

'They're taking us to see the governor,' he whispered to Caradoc and Gwyn. 'It seems

Scapula wants to meet the man he has been fighting against all these years.'

Caradoc was sitting beside them in the wagon with his knees drawn up. He had his head down and his eyes shut, and he didn't respond to Marcus, or give any indication that he had heard him. Marcus opened his mouth to repeat what he had said, but Gwyn gripped Marcus's arm and shook his head, as if to say they should leave Caradoc alone with his thoughts.

Marcus soon lost count of the days they spent on the move. Each one was the same: the jolting of the wagon, the tramp of the soldiers' feet. The legionaries made camp at night, but usually they left the captives in the wagon, giving them only scraps of food and a little water. Eventually they stopped in the legionary fort at Lindum, which Marcus remembered as the place from where his father had written. The thought of that letter still made him angry, but now he felt the cold hand of fear on his heart as well. What if his father was still there?

Marcus and the others were allowed out of the wagon, and then made to line up on the fort's wide parade ground in front of their guards and a group of Roman officers. A centurion yelled harshly at the captives in the British tongue, but with a strong Gaulish accent. 'Kneel before your master, His Excellency the Governor of Britannia, the noble Publius Ostorius Scapula!'

They were slow to do as they were told, and the centurion's men roughly forced them to their knees. It was obvious which of the officers was Scapula – he was at the front of the group, and his armour was far more splendid than anyone else's. He was older than Marcus had expected, with as much grey in his hair as black, but his face was strong, that of a man used to the hard life of a soldier. He stared at Caradoc, his eyes seeming to bore into the chief of the Catuvellauni.

Then Marcus glimpsed his father behind Scapula, and for a terrifying moment he felt as if he couldn't breathe. He quickly lowered his eyes in case his father recognised him. There was a good chance he wouldn't, though – Marcus knew he looked very different from the Roman boy he'd been when his father had last seen him.

Probably all Gaius Arrius Crispus now saw was a dirty barbarian covered in blue tattoos...

'So, Caradoc, we meet at last,' Scapula said in Latin. Caradoc stared back at him, but remained silent. 'What, no great speech – no defiance?' Scapula went on. Caradoc narrowed his eyes slightly, but still said nothing. 'I'm disappointed,' said Scapula. 'But perhaps you are wise to save your words for the emperor in Rome. Oh yes, that's where you're going. Claudius wants to show you off to the people of the city in his triumph... Take them away. I've seen enough.'

They were pulled to their feet again and herded towards the fort's cell block. Marcus glanced over his shoulder and saw that his father was now looking at him with a puzzled expression. Their eyes met briefly, but then Gaius turned to speak to Scapula. Had Marcus been recognised? It seemed not – although, as much as the idea terrified him, he half wished he had. Not to be known by your own father seemed somehow a terrible thing... Then the captives were shoved into a dark, reeking cell, and Marcus tried not to brood about his father any more.

The captives sat in silence, each wrapped in their own thoughts. After a while Marcus lay down to sleep in the filthy straw, and for the first time in years he dreamed of the villa. He was young again, and his mother was there too, sitting on a bench by the fountain in the atrium, waiting for him. But she had the face of Alwen, and Cati was beside her, and they were smiling and beckoning to him, yet he couldn't move. Suddenly he heard his father speak, and they both vanished...

'Wake up, you stinking savage!' someone was yelling. Marcus opened his eyes and saw the centurion from earlier standing above him. The Roman kicked him in the ribs, and two legionaries pulled him to his feet. 'Somebody important wants to have a word with you, my lad.'

Gwyn and several of the other captives were on their feet too, but there was nothing they could do. Another two legionaries were standing by the cell door with their swords drawn, and there were more soldiers in the corridor outside. Marcus looked at Gwyn and their eyes locked together for a moment. Then Marcus was dragged away and the cell door was slammed shut.

* * *

Night had fallen and the sky was black above the fort, and the only light was coming from the red flames of the torches held by a couple of the legionaries. They marched Marcus across the parade ground to a building on the far boundary, and then went inside. The centurion knocked on a door.

'Enter!' said a voice, and Marcus recognised it instantly, his heart sinking.

The centurion opened the door and went in, pulling Marcus with him. 'Is this the savage you wanted to see, Your Honour?' he said. 'To be honest, they all look much the same to me.'

Marcus's father was sitting on a stool beside a small table. He was reading a papyrus roll, and there were more piled on the table and the floor beside him. A narrow military bed stood against one wall, and an old wooden chest that Marcus remembered from the villa stood against another. But otherwise the room was empty.

'Yes, that's him,' Gaius said. 'You may leave us now, Centurion.'

'Are you sure, Your Honour?' said the centurion. 'He might be dangerous...'

'Quite sure. You can go, and close the door behind you.'

The centurion shrugged and did as he was ordered. For a moment there was silence in the room. Marcus kept his head down, but he knew his father was raking him with his eyes.

'I cannot believe such a thing has happened,' Gaius spluttered at last, his voice filled with horror. 'My own son turned into a tattooed savage! You have brought shame upon your country and your family. You have brought shame upon *me*. What do you have to say, boy?'

'I do not understand you, old man,' Marcus muttered in the tongue of the Britons.

'Speak Latin!' Gaius hissed. 'I know it's you, Marcus – I saw it immediately, although I couldn't admit it to myself. You've changed, but you look so much like your mother.'

'Do I?' said Marcus, raising his head and switching to Latin, the words feeling strange and familiar in his mouth at the same time. 'I am glad of it. I hope I don't look like you at all.'

His father scowled and leaned forward. 'Be very careful how you speak to me, Marcus. I could call back the centurion and have him cut your throat. Is that what you want?'

'What else is there for me? You Romans kill all those who stand against you,' said Marcus.

A cloud of anger passed across his father's face, but Gaius brought himself under control. 'You were a Roman once too,' he said, in the clipped tones Marcus remembered. 'And I would like you to tell me how you became what you are now. All I know is that you were captured by the savages – they sent a message to the governor, trying to exchange you for some hostages.'

'And you sent me a letter telling me to kill myself like Cato,' said Marcus.

'As any good Roman father would have done in the circumstances,' said Gaius. 'I agreed with Scapula that we simply could not give in to Caratacus. Why did you not obey my wishes?'

'Because I wanted to live, Father! I had begun to see how good life can be.'

'You think these savages have a good life? They live in mud huts, they worship strange gods, they squabble and fight each other continually. Only we Romans are truly civilized.'

'But Rome abandoned me, Father, and those *savages* gave me a home,' said Marcus.

Silence fell between them once more, and Marcus could see that his father was thinking. At last Gaius took a deep breath, then let it out slowly.

'Well, that is all in the past,' he said. 'But I'm prepared to forgive you for your disobedience and do my best to save you, although it will be difficult and I will have to call in some favours. We can say you were forced to become a savage, and that you've come to your senses now... It would be very useful if you had been tortured.'

'No, Father, I don't want you to do that,' Marcus said, shaking his head, hardly able to believe what he had just heard. 'I swear I would rather die than be a Roman again. So you might as well call the centurion back and get him to cut my throat.'

'Now listen, Marcus – don't be too hasty,' said Gaius. 'You have to realise that if you reject my offer I won't be able to protect you. Things will just have to take their course...'

Marcus was puzzled. He couldn't work out why his father was looking so worried. Surely the noble Gaius Arrius Crispus was the one with all the power in this situation? Then finally Marcus understood, and for an instant he almost felt sorry for the man sitting before him.

'The answer is still no,' he said. 'And you need not worry. I will not reveal I am your son, whatever happens to me, and I will make sure none of the other captives do either.'

His father stared at him, and then turned his head away. 'Very well,' he said quietly, his expression a mixture of relief and embarrassment. 'It seems there is nothing more to say.'

Gaius summoned the centurion and told him to take Marcus back to the cell block. Marcus glanced round as the centurion roughly shoved him out of the door. His father was already reading the roll of papyrus on the table in front of him, a look of intense concentration on his face.

Marcus never saw him again.

CHAPTER ELEVEN
A Fine Speech

That night, Marcus slept more soundly than he had done for a long time, despite the reek of the filthy straw in the cell and the snores of his companions. He woke at first light, the warm sun reaching through the bars of the cell's high window to touch his face. A strange feeling filled him, a peculiar kind of lightness he had never experienced before, and suddenly he realised what it was. He might be locked in this stinking cell and chained to the wall, but Marcus felt free.

His father had been a shadow over his life for as long as he could remember, even after he had come to Britannia, even after he had been adopted by Dragorix and Alwen and had become a warrior of the Catuvellauni. He'd thought he had emptied himself of everything Roman, but his father's voice had always been in the back of his mind, and in his dreams. Last night's conversation had changed things forever, and that voice had finally been silenced.

His joy at the feeling soon faded, though. The captives were dragged from the cell and thrown back onto the wagon to continue the journey south. Nobody had much to say – the only sounds were the creaking of the wagon's wheels and the stamping of the legionaries, although Marcus could tell Gwyn was brooding about something. 'What will they do to us after the emperor has shown us off in his triumph?' Gwyn said eventually. 'Will they sell us as slaves?'

Marcus had translated Scapula's words for the captives who couldn't speak Latin. He had also explained what a triumph was.

A victorious commander was allowed to lead his troops through the streets of Rome, past huge crowds of cheering people. Behind the troops would be wagons of looted treasure and a column of prisoners from the campaign, all of them in chains. It was a chance for the Romans to enjoy a sense of power over those they had defeated.

'Perhaps,' Caradoc said gloomily. 'But it's more likely they will kill us.'

Marcus felt a hot wave of anger. He had grown tired of Caradoc's refusal to speak, but he wished his chief could take back the few words of cold despair he had just uttered. 'Have you no comfort or hope for your followers, Caradoc?' he said. 'That's what we need from you.'

'No, Marcus – I am sorry, but I do not,' said Caradoc, shaking his head sadly. 'I tried to fight the Romans and I lost. I ask myself what I could have done differently, but I have no answers, and I will feel the shame of my failure for as long as I live in this world, and in the next world too. Think of me no longer as your clan chief or as a great warrior – I am Caradoc of the Broken Spear. All I have left is my defiance, and Scapula was right – there will be another time and place for that.'

Caradoc would say no more, and Marcus's anger drained away. Now he understood, and he could not find it in his heart to blame Caradoc for his silence or his words. But Marcus refused to accept there was no hope. He remembered how he had felt when he had read his father's letter – the prospect of death had made him realise how much he wanted to live. Now that feeling surged through him again. Death might be waiting in Rome, but he would do everything in his power to avoid it. He was determined to return to find Alwen and Cati as well, if they were still alive.

He sat up straighter, squared his shoulders, and set his mind to thinking about what he could do to save himself and the others. He would have to come up with some kind of plan...

* * *

There were no opportunities to escape during the journey. They were kept in the wagon and closely guarded all the way from Lindum to Rutupiae. They were then put straight on a ship to Gaul, and in Gesoriacum they were transferred to another wagon, with more guards. Six long weeks later, after another spell in a ship from Narbo, they arrived in Ostia and were taken to Rome.

Marcus looked out at the city through the gaps between the slats of the wagon. It was familiar, of course, but after his years in the hills and woods and fields of Britannia it was strange too. He supposed he was looking at it with different eyes now – the eyes of a foreigner.

Their journey came to an end at last and they were ordered out of the wagon. Marcus and the other captives blinked in the hot Roman sun that beat down onto the parade ground of a huge legionary barracks in the east of the city. Then they were marched to a cell block identical to the one in Lindum, although it contained a surprise. Caradoc's wife and daughters were already there, waiting for him. They ran to Caradoc, and the four of them held each other for a long time.

From that moment on, Caradoc began to return to his old self. Marcus and the other British captives were kept imprisoned in the cell block for a week, but Caradoc looked after them, encouraged them and spoke up for them whenever the guards were late bringing their food or were too brutal. Soon even the guards themselves were treating Caradoc as a great leader who deserved honour and respect. It was good to see, and Marcus felt guilty that he had ever doubted him.

On the day of the triumph, the guards took the captives back to the parade ground, where a crowd of other prisoners was waiting. It seemed that people from the other tribes defeated by the Romans – the Parisi, the Silures, the Ordovices – had been held elsewhere. It took a while to organise everyone into a column, but eventually the order was given to set off. The captives left the barracks, with lines of legionaries in full battle gear marching on both sides of the column.

'Heads up, everybody, and do not be afraid,' said Caradoc. 'Let us show them what it means to be of the Catuvellauni, the greatest tribe of all. Remember, we are a proud people.'

Marcus squared his shoulders again and lifted his chin, and so did the others. They walked on, ignoring the crowds of cheering, jeering Romans lining the streets. More legionaries joined the column, and then the wagons heaped with loot, and finally the emperor Claudius himself, in a fine chariot pulled by two white horses and driven by a slave. The emperor wore a laurel-leaf crown and a golden breastplate, which glittered in the sunlight, and a cloak the colour of blood.

After a while they arrived at the forum, a large open space surrounded by temples and other important buildings, their white columns gleaming. On the far side was a raised platform bearing the emperor's magnificent throne. Claudius stepped down from his chariot, took his seat, and waved at the crowd. The captives were made to stand before him, and a centurion from his personal bodyguard read out a list of the emperor's victories in Britannia from a long scroll.

Marcus's attention had drifted; his eyes were scanning the forum for escape routes, and his mind was full of schemes and plans. But then something happened that brought him up sharply. He heard Caradoc calling out, his voice echoing off the buildings. 'Emperor of the Romans! I have something to say.'

The centurion faltered and fell silent, glancing at the emperor. Claudius looked curious, then shrugged and nodded, gesturing for Caradoc to continue. Caradoc stared at him for a moment, then spoke again, his voice ringing out.

'Once I had wealth and warriors, a home and a hearth, but you have taken all that from me, even though you are so rich and powerful you have need of nothing more. Now I stand here before you, stripped of every weapon but my voice...'

Marcus listened enthralled as Caradoc poured out his defiance. The crowd was hostile at first, yelling and booing, but Caradoc's sheer dignity and courage and pride gradually began to win them round. By the time he had finished speaking most of them were clearly on his side.

'That was a fine speech, one that deserves more than death as its reward,' said the emperor, leaning forward on his throne, a smile playing around his lips. 'Tell me, if I grant you and your family and friends your lives, would you swear never to revolt against Rome again?'

Caradoc turned to look at his wife and daughters and the other captives. Marcus half hoped he would say no, that he would swear the opposite. But he knew that couldn't be.

'I would,' said Caradoc, turning back to the emperor.

The crowd cheered, and Marcus smiled too.

* * *

The emperor did spare their lives, and gave Caradoc and his family and friends a house to live in on the Palatine Hill, near the imperial palace. But the captives from the other tribes were sold in the slave market, and the emperor's gift to Caradoc turned out not to be quite as good as it had seemed. For the great chief was not allowed to return to Britannia, despite his oath.

'It just goes to show that you can never trust a Roman,' Gwyn said bitterly. He and Marcus were sitting with Caradoc in the garden of the house on a sunny afternoon a few weeks later. Far below them lay the city, a distant buzz of noise rising from its busy streets. Two legionaries stood at the garden gate, and Marcus knew that more were stationed at the front of the house.

'I expected nothing less,' said Caradoc, shrugging. 'The emperor has shown himself to be merciful, but he has also made sure that I will never be a threat to Rome again.'

'Perhaps he is not so clever,' said Marcus. 'What if we were to escape? I know the city well – I'm sure I could find us a way out, and we could make it back to Britannia...'

Caradoc smiled at him. 'It would not work, Marcus – we are too many, and even if we managed to get past the guards we would be recognised somewhere. You forget, all Rome saw us in the triumph, and I have my family to think of. The emperor might not be so merciful to us a second time. But you and Gwyn might do it, and something tells me that you have a plan.'

Now it was Marcus's turn to smile. 'You know me too well, Caradoc,' he said. 'I was once a Roman, and I have been thinking it might be useful to be one again, at least for a time...'

It took a while to prepare – to find the right clothes, to acquire enough Roman gold for a long journey and, most importantly, to work out the best time and method for evading the guards. But the day came at last, a day of farewells and blessings, and of escape from the house on the Palatine Hill. Later that afternoon, a young noble Roman arrived at the port of

Ostia with his personal body slave and asked, in his impeccable Latin, which ships were bound for Narbo.

'I can give you passage, if you have the money to pay me,' said a captain they met in a tavern. He was older, his dark hair shot with grey, his face tanned and lined, his eyes shrewd. He spoke Latin well, but the young Roman noticed his accent. The captain was Greek.

'I have enough,' said Marcus in the captain's own tongue. 'When do we sail?'

Marcus thought of his father, and old Stephanos, and smiled to himself.

* * *

Two months later, just as winter was turning to spring, Marcus and Gwyn rode at last down a narrow track and into a small village on the horses they had bought with the last of their Roman money. They had come to the far north of Britannia, and were beyond the power of

Rome. They stopped outside a roundhouse, and two figures emerged from inside as they dismounted: a woman and a girl. It was Alwen and Cati, of course, and the four of them hugged each other.

'Where have you been, Marcus?' said Cati at last. 'What took you so long?'

'Oh, this and that,' he said, ruffling her dark hair. He could see now just how much she looked like her father, and for a moment he saw Dragorix in his mind again. He promised his stepfather's spirit that he would take care of her. 'We'll tell you all about it one day.'

He looked at the roundhouses, the bare rocky hills beyond the village, the grey skies that promised days of cold and mist and rain. And he looked at the people he loved.

It felt good to be home.

Historical Note

As far as we know, Caradoc – or, as the Romans called him, Caratacus – really did exist. He was mentioned by several Roman historians as the chief of the Catuvellauni, and the leader of British resistance to Roman invasion. The Romans defeated the Catuvellauni and the other tribes of the south-east, and Caradoc continued the resistance from the west. He was eventually defeated in battle and fled to Cartimandua of the Brigantes, who handed him over to the Romans.

The story about Caradoc's speech to the emperor was told by the famous Roman historian

Tacitus. He lived in Rome only a few years after the events described in *Revolt Against the Romans,* so he would have talked to people who might well have met the British chief. In fact, he might even have met Caradoc himself. Tacitus also wrote about Calgacus, another British chieftain, who said of the Romans: 'they plunder, slaughter and steal… they make a desert and they call it peace.'

Cartimandua of the Brigantes, Publius Ostorius Scapula and the emperor Claudius all existed too, but Marcus, his father and all the other characters are completely fictional. The Romans spoke Latin, and it's true that the sons of noble Roman fathers were usually taught to speak Greek, the second language of the empire. But the British did have their own language as well. They spoke an old form of a language that still lives today: Welsh, or *Cymraeg* as it's more properly called.

GLOSSARY
OF PLACE NAMES

Batavia	Northern Holland
Gaul	France
Gesoriacum	Boulogne (in France)
Lindum	Lincoln (in Lincolnshire, England)
Narbo	Narbonne (in France)
Ostia	The port of Rome, now a suburb of the city
Rutupiae	Richborough (in Kent, England)
Sabrina	The River Severn
Tamesis	The River Thames
Verulamium	St Albans (in Hertfordshire, England)